THE HIP HOP CHESSMASTER

ROLAND P. TAYLOR

Illustrations by Bethany Root

Copyright © 2017 Roland P. Taylor
All rights reserved
First Edition

PAGE PUBLISHING, INC.
New York, NY

First originally published by Page Publishing, Inc. 2017

ISBN 978-1-68409-105-8 (Paperback)
ISBN 978-1-68409-106-5 (Digital)

Printed in the United States of America

FOREWORD

Vaughn is a popular kid in school because of his lyrical prowess, but no one knows his secret passion for the art of chess. One day, his worlds collide when he must make a choice—perform at the school talent show with his crew or attend the regional championship chess match.

Can he live in both worlds and still keep the respect from his friends and his family?

The *Hip-Hop Chess Master* is the tale of a young, middle school boy who finds himself torn between two loves—hip-hop and chess. What will he decide? Be a rapper? Be a chess player? Or truly become… the hip-hop chess master.

OPENING

Hi, my name is Vaughn. Some people know me as MC Paunzi. However, there is another side—a side of me that most people don't know. This is my story…

"A, yes yes y'all, and ya don't stop. MC Paunzi and ya don't stop. A, yes yes y'all, and ya don't stop. MC Paunzi will be the sure shot—come on!

"Man, Dad, I really love that old school hip-hop sound. 'I used to love H.E.R.' by Common Sense is so cool! I can most definitely use that in my flow. It's what makes me different from the rest of the rappers out here nowadays… that touch of old-school flavor," said Vaughn.

"I have to tell you son, you remind me of myself when I was your age, and I'm glad that you have discovered this talent. But I don't want hip-hop to totally consume you. I want you to be a well-rounded young man," Dad said affectionately. "Take your chess, for example, it's what makes you different, and in a good way. I know it isn't the 'cool' thing to do, but it's something that was passed down from Gramps to me, and now from me to you. It's a Robinson tradition."

"You mean, like you passing down hip-hop to me?" asked Vaughn.

"Hmmm… sort of," Dad replied. Don't get me wrong, son, I love hip-hop, but I also know that chess can open up so many more opportunities for you. It trains your mind to think strategically and provokes a totally unique approach to how you conduct yourself in stressful and competitive situations. Plus, look at how good you are. I mean, they don't give away all of those trophies you have in your room to just anyone!"

"Yeah, Dad, I hear you," answered Vaughn. "To me, hip-hop is the same. It exercises the creative side of the brain. Not only is it entertaining, but it really helps me with building my vocabulary and makes me want to read more. In fact, I sometimes find myself reading the dictionary just to make my rhymes more intense!"

"And also to get your English grades up too, correct?" Dad interrupted.

"Of course, of course," said Vaughn. "Trust me, Dad, I know how important school is. Hip-hop and chess are both things that I care about, and I know that if I let my grades slip… well, let's just say I don't plan on letting that happen!"

"So, son, if chess is so important to you, and you are that good at it, then why won't you tell your friends and share it with them just like you do hip-hop, MC Paunzi?" asked Dad with a smirk.

"Dad, I guess it's like the Fresh Prince said, '*Parents just don't understand*,'" said Vaughn.

"Wow, son, I really have to stop letting you listen to my old-school tapes," Dad chuckled.

"No way!" said Vaughn. "I told you, that's what makes my hip-hop style special and different. Besides, my friends wouldn't understand chess. They are more into sports like football, basketball, and baseball. I like all of those, but even if they found out that I was good at chess, I still don't think they would truly accept it."

"And that is why we always go to tournaments out of town?" Dad asked.

"Exactly! It would totally ruin my rep!" Vaughn replied.

"Your what?" asked Dad. He continued, "Son, you're only twelve years old. You haven't lived long enough to have a rep." Dad looked at Vaughn and saw himself in his adolescent child. Thinking better than to give his son another lecture, he instead gently placed his hand on Vaughn's shoulder. "Hey, it's getting late and you have school tomorrow. Head to bed, and I will see you in the morning. "I love you, my hip-hop chess master."

"I love you too, Dad!" said Vaughn. As he lay in his bed, he thought about what his dad said. He thought it would be nice if he felt his friends accepted him for his love of chess like they did his lyrical skills. But all of that aside, Vaughn had two things on his mind—tomorrow's math test and the school talent show coming up in two weeks. He has been working on this song for a few months in preparation for the said event and was very anxious to perform it in front of his classmates… especially Sherry.

Vaughn walked bleary-eyed down the crowded hallway filled to the brim with dozens of voices strung together like knotted electrical wires. With every couple of steps, he honed in on a conversation, but was too foggy to listen on. Vaughn didn't remember the ride to school, but seeing Mike towering over everyone at the end of the hallway signaled that he was there. Rodney Matthews accidentally steps on the back of his tennis shoes, followed by a "my bad." He didn't even look behind him.

No sooner had he stuffed his heel back into his sneaker did he see Chris Chambers, his best friend. "Yo, Vaughn! What's up, man?" shouts Chris. "You ready for this killer math test today? I've been sweating it all weekend!"

Vaughn gathered himself enough to reply, "Yeah, I'm pretty sure I'm ready for it, but I have bigger things to worry about," said Vaughn

"Like what?"Chris asked

"Like what? Like the spring talent show, that's what!" replied Vaughn.

"Man, come on, you know no one here can touch your flow. Everybody is doing that same tired stuff we all hear on the radio. But you… you are different. It's good and it works. Plus, during lunch you always win the freestyle battles," Chris ranted.

"Not the last one," Vaughn said, disheartened.

"Yeah, but that was luck. Everyone thinks Troy [MC Amazin'] wrote that beforehand just waiting for the chance to face you. Don't even sweat it. You know you're the best. Let me hear some of what you've got prepared for the show.

"All right?" said Vaughn.

"It's a new concept, but I'm going to let you peep a little bit of it. So here we go." Vaughn began to bop his head to a beat only he could hear. As if on cue, he…

Now in life you have to make moves like a chess game.

You always have to think three moves ahead.

Even pawns have a role to play if you want to remain.

And if not, you hear a "checkmate" losing instead—*checkmate!*

Chris stood in amazement. "Vaughn, as always, that was hot! But what's up with the chess game stuff? I don't get it? You don't even play chess."

It's so weird, Vaughn thought to himself. *This is my best friend, but I don't feel like I can confide in him, or any other person, that my second passion next to hip-hop is chess. I mean, he's my boy and he should have my back no matter what. But can I take that chance? I have a good thing going here at school with my rapping. No issues from the older kids because they respect my flow. And the girlies dig me because I stand out by doing something cool. I can do something that not a lot of other kids in school can do—at least not as well, in my opinion, as me. They like that you know, the girlies! But only if it's something cool.*

For example, take Charles Taylor. He is cool because he always has the latest pair of Jordans. It's so hard to believe that Jordans are still so insanely popular since my father talked about having them when he was my age… eons ago!

I mean, I remember people wanted the latest design so badly that they camped outside of the shoe store overnight, and at one mall, they actually caused a riot. Incredible! And Charles has to have, like, fifty pairs!

Then there is Mike Kepner. Mike plays for our basketball team. He's only a sixth grader, but he is a starter on our basketball team, and I know he's got to be at least six feet, four inches easily. He is taller than any of the other kids in school and even most of the teachers—all but Mr. Brooks, our gym teacher. Rumor has it Mr. Brooks used to play in the NBA but got hurt after only three years and had to retire. Mr. Brooks is six feet, eight inches and can touch the basketball rim without even jumping. He's always telling us about the importance of finishing school because "You never know what life may throw your way." He and my father went to school together and whenever he catches me freestyling, he says that I remind him of my father who had a hip-hop group back in the day. Mr. Brooks is mad cool.

But back to Mike. He's been playing B-ball since he was about five. It's so funny because he always carries a basket-

ball with him wherever he goes—books in one hand, basketball in the other. It's funny, but you have to respect him for his dedication. He's one of the best players in the county, and every once in a while, you will see college scouts at our games. College scouts!? Man, that is crazy! So naturally, the girls flock to him. See, he's… *different*, but in a cool way.

There is, however, one exception to this rule at school, Barry McKinley. Barry is a certifiable, undeniable *nerd*. Not that there is anything wrong with being a nerd, I'm not saying that at all. But if you look up *nerd* in the dictionary, you might see his face. I mean, quiet, glasses, and always wears his shirts tucked in and buttoned all of the way up to the top. He's a sixth grader just like me.

But here's the reason why this guy gets attention from the girlies… he's famous! Yep, world famous in fact! And I'm not talking famous because he has won all of the Math 24 contests since fourth grade countywide. Or the fact that he always wins first place in our STEM fairs. I can remember when he won in our last year of elementary school. He built this life-sized, voice-activated, LEGO robot that looked just

like President Obama. It was freaky how real it looked! Barry even got the opportunity to travel to Washington, DC, to show the robot to the president.

But that is not why he is world famous. Nope! Barry is world famous because outside of all of these accomplishments, Barry has a very unique talent. He has memorized the number pi. You know, March 14, 3.14 (the ratio of a circle's circumference to its diameter). I didn't think it was such a big deal until I looked it up on the Internet. It turns out that memorizing pi is an international phenomenon. They have all kinds of categories and age ranges. The actual calculation of pi is infinite. I think a computer was able to count up to five trillion digits. The world record holder is from China, and he was able to memorize over sixty-seven thousand digits! It took him just over a whole day to recite the string of numbers. That is almost unbelievable if it hadn't really happened.

Barry isn't the world record holder. However, he does hold the North American record for memorizing the most digits of pi for his age range—the eleven to sixteen bracket.

He received a huge trophy and $5,000! I couldn't believe it. That is a *ton* of money for a kid our age. I know that Charles probably kept thinking of how many pairs of Jordan he could buy with that money. I was so impressed that I actually tried to start memorizing pi. But the highest I got to was twenty digits. Barry actually memorized three hundred digits!

Although he won the $5,000, his parents only let him spend $100 of it. The rest went into a college fund. I mean, I know college is important from everything my parents say, but man, what a bummer! Taking the time to memorize all of those numbers for just $100? Just doesn't seem fair.

But Barry got more than prize money that day… he got noticed: by the teachers, by the other kids in school, and now surprisingly enough… by the girlies! But this is rare, and more than likely, would never happen. Without these accolades, Barry would be in the category they put school safeties, tutors, and kids in the chess club… the "uncool zone"!

This is a zone I have tried hard to stay out of, especially being at the bottom of the totem pole in middle school as a sixth grader.

Now you see my dilemma. Not only could I not tell my best friend Chris, but anyone for that matter. If anyone discovered that I was a "chessy"—

"Chessy": (def.) a kid in the Chess Club that no one feels comfortable talking to because they always relate everything back to a chess game. The epitome of uncool!

It could potentially erase all the positive reputation I've built up with my rhyming skills. And that rep would disappear fast! Faster than that guy who jumped from space and broke the sound barrier *fast*!

I could see it now. The news would roll throughout the school quicker and more thunderous than an avalanche. They would make an announcement over the school intercom system, "Attention, all students. MC Paunzi plays chess and shall now and forever be stripped of his cool status!"

Instead of people cheering at the sound of my lyrical skills, their mouths would now fall mute. No clapping, just laughing and jeering. It would be a nightmare! And worse of all Troy, MC Amazin' would now reign as the top MC in the school. I could never let that happen! And so my secret passion for chess will remain intact.

BIND

"Hey, Vaughn," called Dad.

"Yeah, Dad?"

"Come down here for a second. I have something to share with you," Dad called from the kitchen.

"All right, be down in a minute," I yelled from downstairs.

Vaughn was working on an idea for the show before his dad called him. There were some kids down at the mall that had their own break-dancing group. They usually performed on weekends right outside of the food court for any spare change shoppers were willing to give them. From the looks of the baseball caps that they placed on the ground surrounding their makeshift dance floor, it doesn't look like they bring home much money. If you then split that money between about five guys and three girls, that really doesn't leave much per person. But I guess, like me, they do it for love—the love of hip-hop. These kids were good too! They made it to the second to last round on *Battle Crews*, a nationally televised dance contest where crews from all over the nation compete to determine the best street dance team.

Hip-hop isn't just about MC'ing. It also involves break-dancing and graffiti art. They all work together in harmony—almost like an ecosystem, all parts relying on each other to survive. These are the types of people I need for my show. I know that they can take my performance to the next level! My rhymes… their dance moves… nothing but perfection! Plus, I can't afford to pay them so the fact that they dance for pennies really works to my benefit. I'll have to approach them with the idea next time I'm at the mall. Besides, I need to go there anyway to look for an outfit for the show.

I'll also stop by to see my grandfather at the Senior Living Center. It's about time for our monthly chess game. Gramps is really getting up there in age, so we never finish a game during one visit. In fact, we've been playing this current game for the past three months—slowly and methodically. I usually don't have that much patience when I play but this is Gramps, so I don't mind making the exception.

My grandfather always has some wisdom to drop on me no matter what situation I present to him. One time I asked

him what I should do to get the attention of Sherry Campbell, one of the prettiest girls in class and who I've had a crush on since third grade. I told Gramps that she never seemed to notice me, even as MC Paunzi? It just never seemed to impress her. Gramps told me that although he really didn't understand hip-hop and called it a bunch of "noise," he did realize that at the heart of hip-hop is music and poetry. So he told me to drop the MC Paunzi and the music and just be Vaughn with the poetry.

"Write her a poem, Vaughn," Gramps said. "Make it simple and to the point. And most importantly, be yourself."

So I did. The poem went something like this:

> Although you never notice me,
>
> And sometimes it's like I'm not there,
>
> You have been on my mind,
>
> Each year after year.
>
> From third grade till now,

Your beauty remains the same,

Your smile is like the sun,

That can clear up any rain.

I like the way you talk,

And those stylish clothes you wear,

So please don't be offended,

Because I can't help but stare.

And you know what, it worked! Well, at least it did briefly. For one whole week, Sherry and I were boyfriend and girlfriend. But when Barry won that pi contest, she realized that she liked smart guys. And even though I get good grades, come on… how do you compete with international fame? Go figure.

Although it didn't last long, I still appreciated Gramps's advice. He always knew what to say, plus I always walked away with a cool $5 in my pocket!

"Vaughn!" exclaimed his father! "Did you forget that I asked you to come down? I have something important to show you."

"I'm coming down now," I replied. Wow, I got so caught up in thinking about the show and visiting Gramps that I must've been daydreaming. I hurried downstairs. Dad was in the sitting in the kitchen.

"What's going on, Dad?" I asked.

"Check this out," said Vaughn's father. "There's an amateur chess tournament coming up in Alexandria, Virginia, and the grand prize is $1,000 for your age group. I found out about it late, so I had to send in the admission fee right away without asking you about it. But with a $1,000 grand prize, I didn't think you would mind. Plus, it's only about an hour and a half from here."

"No, not at all, Dad, I don't mind. Thanks." Vaughn chuckled. *I just hope I can spend more of the prize money than Barry was able to.*

This really didn't seem like it would be an issue. That is, until I noticed the date. May 15.

OMG! This can't be happening! Now normally this wouldn't be an issue. I mean I'm no stranger to competing in out of town tournaments. That is nothing new. But two Saturdays from now is also the same day as the spring talent show! This is such bad luck, and it is only this year that the school talent show happens to fall on the weekend. It's usually one evening after school, but this year, they had so many participants that they wanted to give everyone who signed up a chance to really display their talents.

So what am I going to do? I'm now committed to both. I've been planning out my performance for the spring talent show for weeks, but I don't want to disappoint my father either. Man, this is crazy! I need to speak to someone who always seems to have the right answer… Gramps!

CHAPTER THREE

ANALYSIS

Seeing Gramps was cool! Although he is eighty years old, he still has all of his wits about him. He never carries himself like he is just another old person in a senior center. Gramps was always laid back and relaxed, but wise and he walks with a fancy, mahogany cane. But don't call it a cane because he is quick to correct you and say that it is a "gentleman's walking stick." Yeah, Gramps is one sharp man. He worked as a banker for years, but now he is more content with living his life to the fullest. Nothing slows him down.

There is also another gentleman who lived in the center that I talked to sometimes. After I finish visiting with Gramps, I always go down the hall to speak to Mr. Grady. He is a little older than my grandfather but still got around pretty well. I normally wouldn't have a reason to visit anyone else in the facility but my grandfather, but since the last talent show at the senior center starring their own residents, everything changed.

There was a lady who used to be an opera singer and another who read her own original poetry. There was also a gentleman who gave his best attempt at a magic show. He

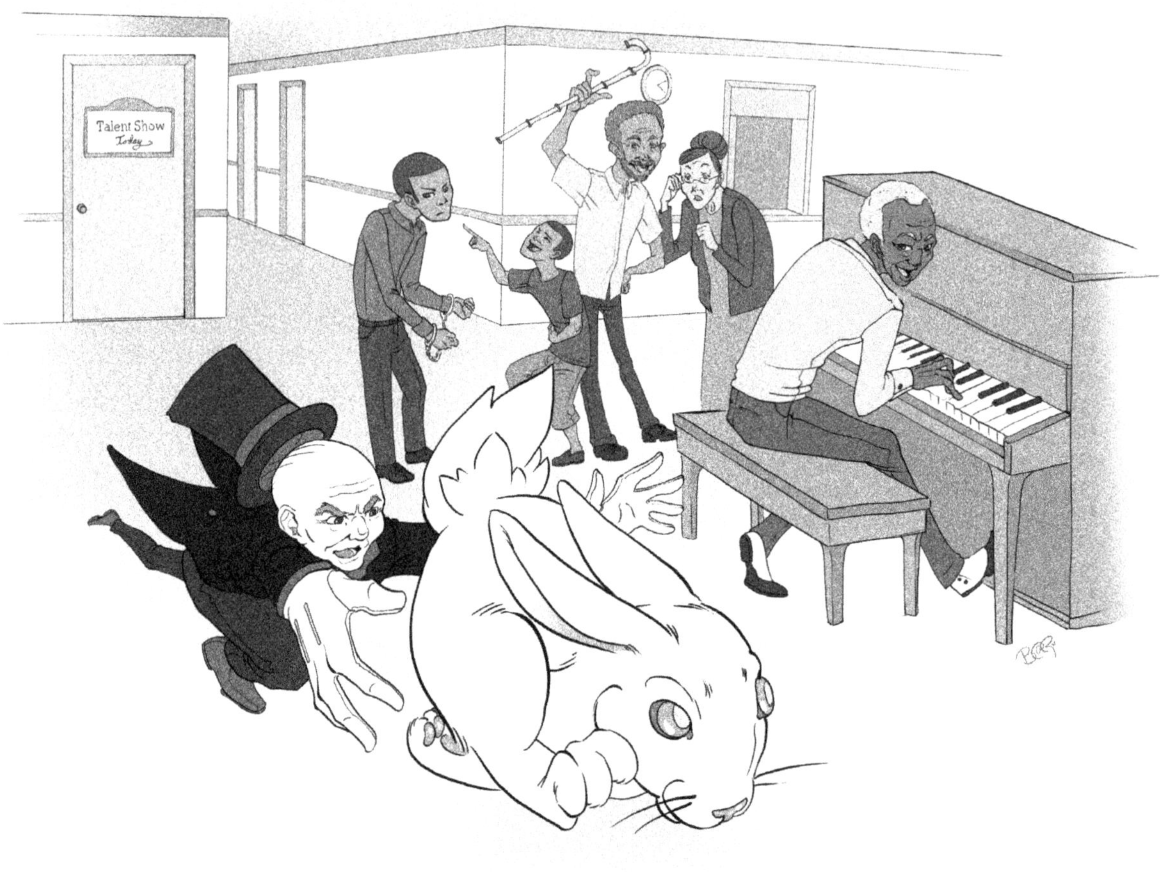
Talent Show
Today

called himself "The Great Randuchi!" But the rabbit he was supposed to make disappear escaped and began hopping all around the lobby where the performers were. Things went from bad to worse when we realized that his fake handcuffs were actually real! It was so funny because he couldn't remember where he had placed the keys. But the humor wore off because after a while, they had to call the police to come and get them off. It took hours, but the experience was amazing!

Then there was Mr. Grady. It turns out that Mr. Grady used to be an old cabaret performer like those from back in the early days when you usually had to sing, dance, and act. We call those people "triple threats" now. He started as a kid when people noticed his talents as a performer. He wasn't nearly as famous as leaders like Cab Calloway, but he did follow his career and modeled his style after him as well as that of other performers like the Nicholas Brothers. So when it was his turn to perform, he didn't hold anything back.

I watched with awe as Mr. Grady played the piano, sang, and did a tap dance routine like you wouldn't believe. I was totally blown away! I just couldn't believe it. My grandfather

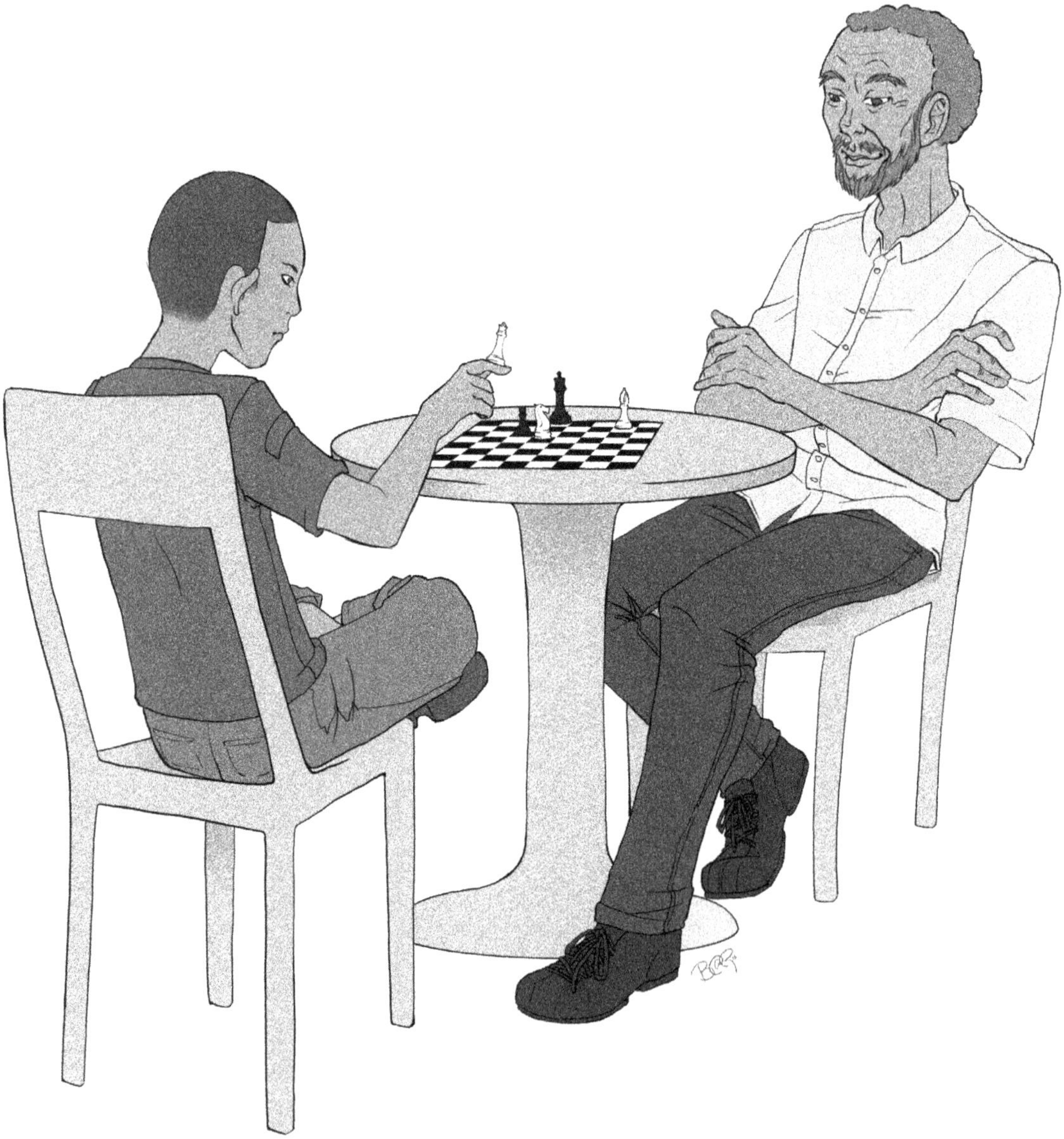

told Mr. Grady that I was somewhat of a performer as well. And since then, I make it my business to drop by to get tips on how to put on a good show.

My time with Gramps is much more of a ritual than a visit. When I sit down with Gramps, the first thing I do is make my next move in our longstanding chess match. (*Move*—hxg5+, a Zwischenzug. Bye-bye, pawns.)

"Check!" I say, gloating.

Grandpa stares at the chess board as if trying to move the pieces with his mind. "Interesting," he said.

He always says that as if to both encourage me and to throw me off at the same time. It used to bother me, but not anymore. Now, my skills have progressed to the point where I enter "the zone"—and when I'm playing in the zone, nothing can throw me off.

"So, Vaughn, what's on your mind?"

I took a deep breath and proceeded. "Gramps, I have a big dilemma!"

"Go on," said Gramps as he makes his move. (*Move—Qxg5.*)

"I have the spring talent show in a few weeks."

"So are you ready?" he asked, still never taking his eyes off the board.

"For sure!" I said. "I just need to work out some last-minute details, but I'm ready."

"So what's your dilemma?" asked Gramps, intrigued.

"Dad signed me up for a chess tournament on the very same day as the talent show. I don't know what to do! I mean, this talent show is very important to me, and I've really been planning for it. Plus it will help me keep my status in school as the top MC."

"The top what? MC?" asked Gramps.

"MC, microphone controller… I'm sorry, Gramps. It's another term for rapper," I explained.

"Boy, I sure don't understand you young folks," Gramps said with a chuckle. "Go on."

"Right—I can't miss this talent show, but I love going to these chess tournaments. Even if I decided to not go to the talent show, no one would ever understand that I gave it up for a just a chess contest," I said.

"What do you mean, just a chess contest? Why do you say it like that?" said Gramps.

"Gramps, no one at school, not even my friends, know I play chess. It's just not something that is very popular," explained Vaughn.

"Well, life is like a chess match, Vaughn. Sometimes the easiest move isn't always the best move. You see, it's very easy to go along with the crowd, but it takes true courage to be a leader and an individual. Besides, have you ever thought that you may be depriving your friends the opportunity of learning something new through chess? This game is more than just moving pieces on squares. It's all about strategy. And now, you must think of a good strategy to help you come to an answer to your dilemma. But no matter what, Vaughn, always be true to who you are!" Gramps said emphatically.

"Thanks, Gramps, and by the way [*move*—Rxh5#] that king isn't going anywhere. Checkmate!"

CHAPTER FOUR

CHECKMATE

Gramps was right, and now I understand. It was just like what Chris said about my rhyming style. Bringing that old-school flavor makes me different—makes me who I am. Now I need to take it to another level. But I'll need Chris's help to make it work. It's going to take perfect timing, teamwork, and a little bit of luck.

It's the day of the tournament and the spring talent show, and I'm ready for both. Dad and I set out for Virginia, and I'm pumped up; my game face is on. The tournament should run until about 6:00 PM.

Dad has already promised to go just a little faster than normal to get me back up to the school after we are done. The vocal music performances should go last, and I've requested that I be one of the later performers. Still, it will be very, very close.

Right before the matches start, I go through my normal prep routine. I don't wear prescription glasses, but I like the look. So one day after coming home from a 3D movie, I decided to alter the glasses. I took a black marker and black-

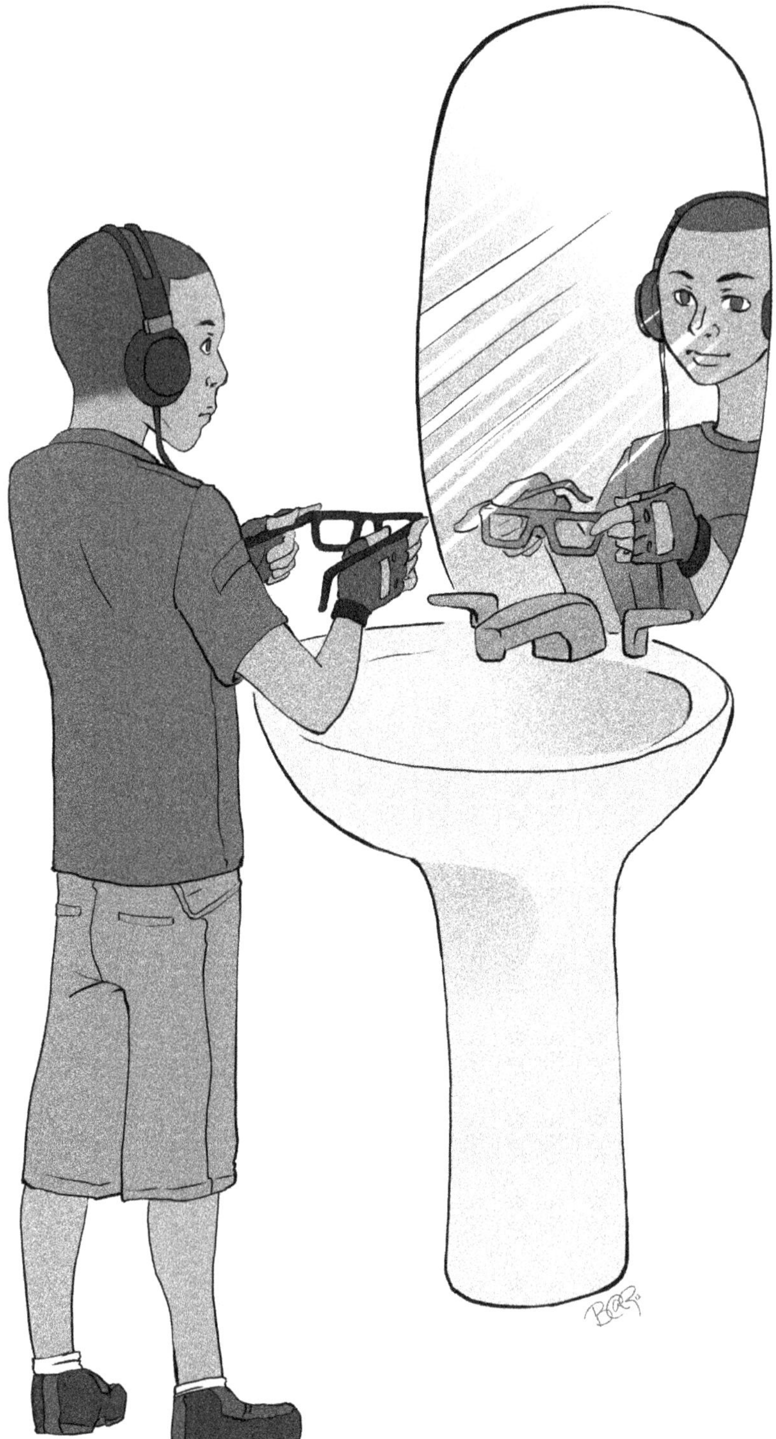

ened out the "3D" writing on the sides. I then pushed out the lens so that all I had left was the plain, black frames. Very cool! So I have my trademark black frames, one black driver's glove that I cut to expose the fingers just for my right hand, and a song I usually listen to by Eric B & Rakim. The title "Know the Ledge" is really a play on the word *knowledge*, which is fundamental when playing chess—well, that and instinct. It's another one of my father's favorites. The beat is up tempo with great bass. The glove is just something I thought looked cool. I wear the same glove when I perform. I'm right-handed, and that is the hand I use to hold the microphone.

I check the time as I move through the rounds—5:30 PM. I have just one more match—the finals! This was a sixteen-player, single-elimination or "knock-out" style tournament. The seeds were based on ratings, and my Elo ranking is pretty high, given my previous victories. This guaranteed that I didn't face the hardest competition until the finals.

This is it! I'm five moves in and looking good. It's funny. So many people assume that chess is just a board game that

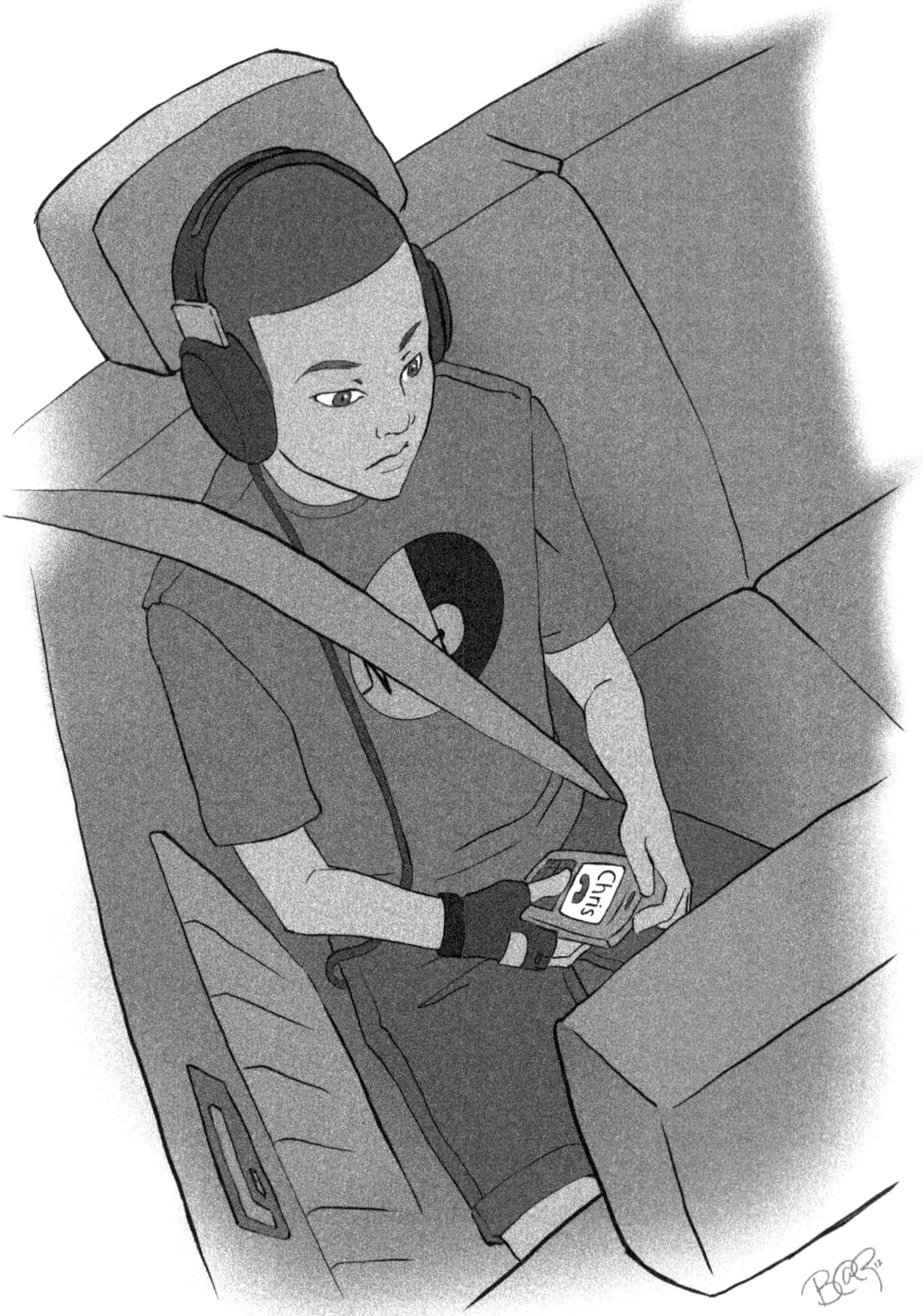
Chris

you sit down and play like checkers. But obviously, these are people who know nothing about the "art of chess." It's like the "Olympics of the mind." To play chess, you really have to work hard and come prepared. Not to mention stamina. You try staying glued in one seat, constantly thinking two, three, four, or even five moves ahead, sometimes for an hour or more? It definitely takes something out of you. But the rewards are worth it. To know that you out-thought, out-witted, and out-lasted your opponent. Well, let's just say it isn't checkers by a *long* shot!

"Check!" That word coming out of my mouth is like a runner about to cross the finish line, like a running back in football with five yards to go to the end zone, or like a center in basketball midair about to catch an alley-oop right before the buzzer. And then it comes, "Checkmate!" Game over. Tournament won and one thousand dollars in my pocket. Now Dad has got to get me back to school. And fast!

We are about fifteen minutes away when Chris shoots me a text: "Vaughn, Troy just finished n killed it! They r asking 4 u. How far away r u?"

I text back, "About 15 min. Stick with the plan n start the show!! CYAL8R."

The lights of the auditorium fade to black. Without warning, the beat starts:

Boom boom dat, boom boom boom boom dat dat, boom dat boom dat, boom boom dat...

Then one single spotlight stretches down to the center of the stage. There, stands a figure in a black hoodie, jeans, and black boots. Black shades covered the mask used to conceal his identity. Slowly, yet purposefully, the figure raises his right hand to the beat. Wearing a black driver's glove with the fingers cut out, he starts swaying back and forth to the beat, microphone in hand, as if he were controlling the crowd like a conductor leads an orchestra.

Boom boom dat, boom boom boom boom dat dat, boom dat boom dat, boom boom dat…

The infectious beat sent the crowd into a frenzy. The chant of "Go, Paunzi! Go, Paunzi!" saturates the auditorium like a soaked sponge. Then all of a sudden, the person on the stage disappears in a puff of smoke… *poof!* The beat continues and a screen drops from the ceiling. An image appears through the static grey fuzz like a TV channel that isn't quite clear. It looks like it is someone dressed the same as the person on stage, moving back and forth to the beat. And then you hear the word "Checkmate" with strategically placed pauses to form a chorus… "Checkmate." The image becomes clearer, and now on the screen it's none other than MC Paunzi. He starts his verse:

Now in life you have to make moves like a chess game,

You always have to think three moves ahead…

The verse resonated just as he had practiced with Chris. The words echoed throughout the school auditorium with profound impact. The lyrics were concise, cleverly and metaphorically comparing the game of chess to convey a message of determination. The verse comes to a close making room for the chorus…

Checkmate. The end of the game is Checkmate.

The outcome depends on the moves that you make.

It's all about the strategy, never doubt yourself. Or else it will end up as a tragedy.

And now the crowd is singing along as if hypnotized. He's done it! Vaughn has managed to make chess… well… cool!

The screen goes blank, the lights turn up, another puff of smoke, and now MC Paunzi makes his appearance from underneath of the stage. But now, it's not just him. He is surrounded by dancers, half in white, the other half in black. The lights have also revealed a life-size chessboard on stage. The dancers are bringing to life a chess game through the artistry of break-dancing! Vaughn was able to get the break dancers from the mall! *Nice*! As the song reaches the end, a second MC Paunzi walks on stage. How can this be? Well, to know that, you have to know the plan.

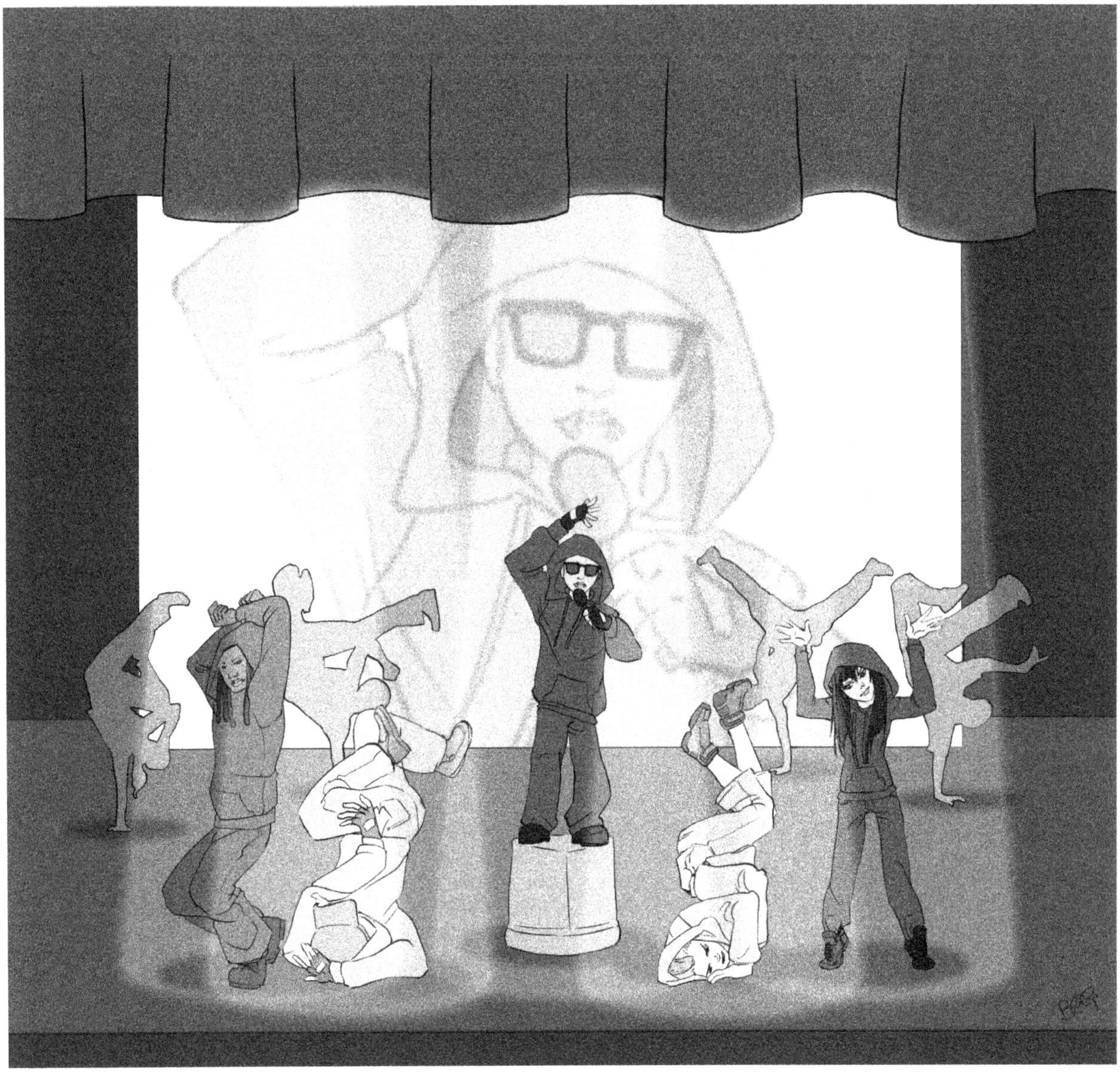

Vaughn knew that there was a strong possibility he wasn't going to make it back in time to start the show. So his strategy was to use his resources. First, he had to enlist the help of his friend Lisa who worked in the technology lab at school. She pre-taped his performance, almost like a Skype message to the crowd. This is what was showing on the big screen during the performance.

He also knew that he needed his boy Chris to help. Chris and Vaughn are about the same height and build, so Vaughn knew that if he had Chris dress up in all black, wear a black mask, and had him wear the trademark driver's glove, then the crowd wouldn't be able to distinguish his identity and would believe that Chris was actually MC Paunzi. All of this put together, afforded Vaughn enough time to get to school, change, and then reappear for the finale! Genius! The icing on the cake was something he learned from the talent show at the Senior Living Center. Thinking back to the Great Randuchi, he knew that adding that element of magic with the smoke would get the crowd's attention. And using the trap door in the stage that the drama club uses in school plays before gave Vaughn the perfect cover.

It was a phenomenal day! I won the chess tournament and also came in first place for the spring talent show. Dad and Gramps were both right. Being who I am and staying true to me ultimately worked. Now I don't have to hide my passion for chess anymore. I can enjoy both openly and freely without worrying about people judging me and not accepting me for who I am. But what is most rewarding is that since my performance, people actually think chess is cool, especially the chessies!

All is right with the world… well not quite all of the world. There was one chink in my elaborate plan. Using Chris as my stand-in for me at the talent show somehow resulted in he and Sherry going steady. Apparently, she thought it was so nice that Chris covered for me at the talent show (never mind that it was *totally* my idea!). Well, I guess you can't win them all—even if you are… *the hip-hop chess master*!

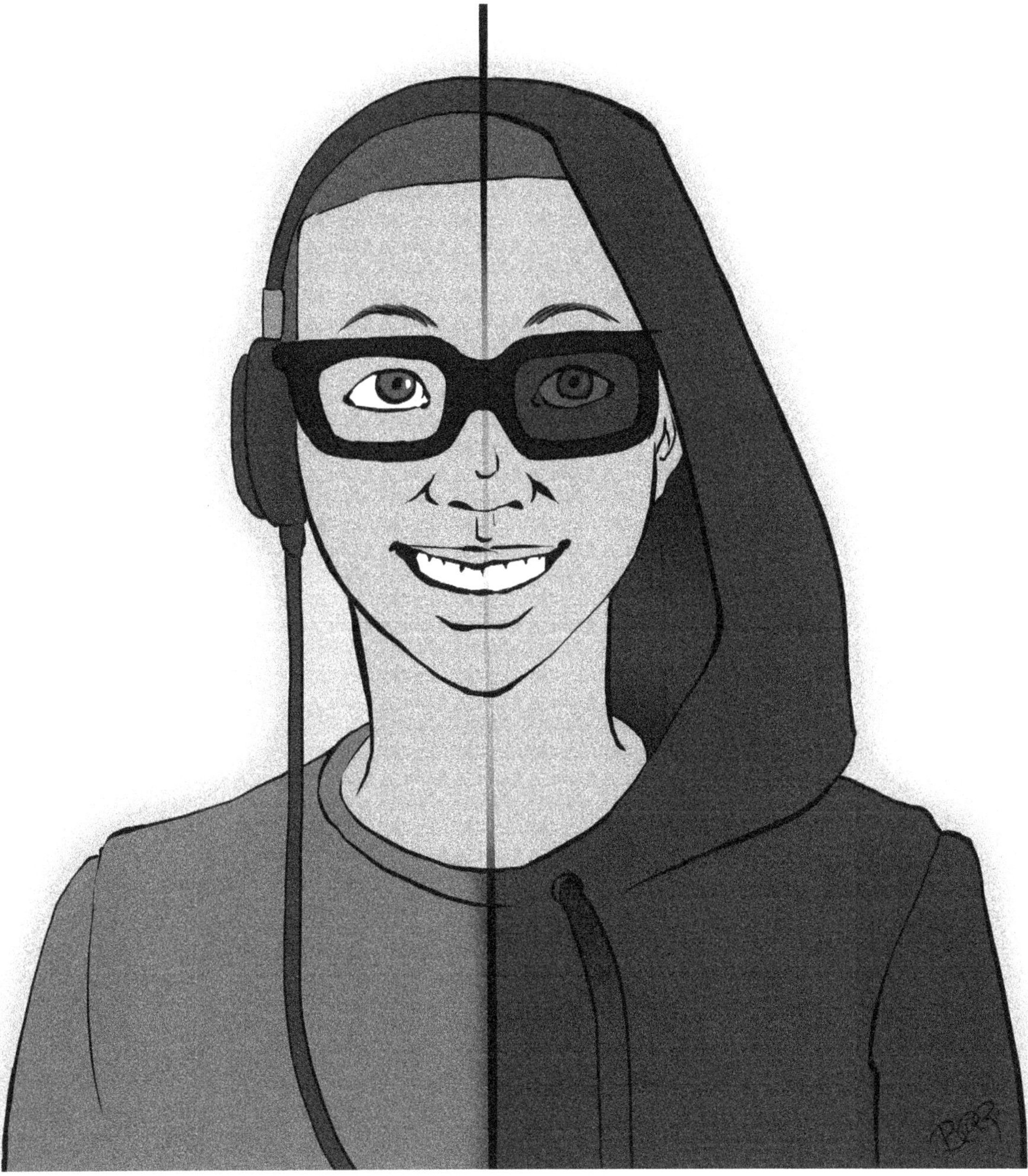

ABOUT THE AUTHOR

Roland Taylor is a first time author, husband, father, education and finance professional, and a life-long hip-hop junkie! The muse for the story centers around family, but most importantly his son. Roland strongly believes in the power of family and the strength in the relationship and bond between father and son. He is also a strong proponent of creativity, the arts, STEM, individuality, and acceptance of all. This book is meant to inspire all children who dare to be different. Dare to dream. Dare to express their talent in spite of public perception. As a child, Roland grew up surrounded by all types of cultures, races, religions, and economic classes. He learned to love rock and hip-hop, skateboarding and basketball, and lived in suburbia as well as the inner city. He understands the importance a father can and should have in a son's life. And that children should be encouraged to embrace differences and not be afraid of them. Roland was born and raised in Baltimore, MD. Ironically, Roland does not play chess. But he is inspired by the dedication and strategic mind-set the game evokes.

CHECKMATE

Written by Roland P Taylor

Chorus:
Checkmate, the end of the game is Checkmate.
The end of the game is Checkmate.
The outcome depends on the moves that you make.
It's all about the strategy, never doubt yourself.
Or else it'll end up as a tragedy.

Verse 1
Now in life you have to make moves like a chess game
You always have to think 3 moves ahead
Even pawns have a role to play if you want to remain
And if not, you hear a "Checkmate" losing instead
So don't you let up, and if you're down boy you better get up
Cause if not, you're gonna get faded like a haircut
And use your head, stay strong don't ever let up
You're thinking that they gave in, but really it's a set up
So don't fall for tricks get set just like a laser
Stay on point and you can be the better player

Chorus (repeat twice)

Verse 2

Here we go time is ticking, you need to make a move
Be smart and confident don't even think that you'll lose
It's a hard decision, be smart and use precision
Cause this is your life, it's not a fantasy or fiction
No contradiction, your dedication is your one prescription
So follow your direction, don't keep your talent hidden
Never ever forbidden, cause it's your life you're living
So stay balanced and you will never find yourself slipping
Cause this is your time to shine bright
The energy of positivity will be your guiding light

Chorus (repeat twice)
Scratch interlude

Verse 3

So you can choose to be a follower or choose to be a leader
Choose to be a giver or become a receiver
But maybe you can be whatever makes you successful

As long as you're true your life will be less stressful
So never back down and never give up on your dreams
Cause everything in life isn't always what it seems
Just like magic, living your life as an illusion is tragic
A terrible habit so get back at it
The truth is what counts so you should make it your reality
Never let them call you a fake living a fallacy

Chorus (repeat once)

Outro

It's all about the strategy
Never give up on your dreams
It's all about the strategy
Never give up on your dreams

Now, you can experience music from the book including the tracks "Checkmate" and "Lunchroom Battle". Just visit https://soundcloud.com/thehiphopchessmaster